FERGUS'S
UPSIDE-DOWN DAY

Phototypeset by Spooner Graphics, London NW5
Printed and bound in Belgium by Proost
for the publishers, Piccadilly Press Ltd.,
5 Castle Road, London NW1 8PR

A catalogue record for this book is available from the British Library

Tony Maddox lives in Worcestershire. Piccadilly Press publish his tremendously successful books, *Spike, the Sparrow Who Couldn't Sing* and his first Fergus book, *Fergus the Farmyard Dog*.

FERGUS'S

UPSIDE-DOWN DAY

Tony Maddox

Piccadilly Press · London

"We're off to market, Fergus!"
called Farmer Bob.
"Look after the animals and make sure
they don't get into any trouble."

"A nice quiet day!" thought Fergus. "Nothing to do but sleep in the sun." He looked around. The hens were in the yard, the ducks were by the pool and the pigs were in their pen.

In the orchard, the goat was looking
for fallen apples and the cow was grazing
in the meadow.

All seemed well.
"I think I'll bury my bone behind
the barn," thought Fergus.

But when he returned sometime later,
there was no sign of the hens, or the ducks,
or the pigs, or the goat, or the cow!

Then he noticed the open farmhouse door!
He looked inside to see the hens
and the ducks . . . watching television!

He went through to the kitchen.
There were the pigs . . . eating spaghetti
and baked beans!

He rushed upstairs to the bedroom
to find the goat . . . wearing the new
hat and coat that Farmer Bob's wife
had just bought!

And when he opened the bathroom door,
he couldn't believe his eyes . . .

. . . the cow was taking a bubble bath!

Suddenly the clock struck four! Farmer Bob
and his wife would be back at any moment!
"Woof, Woof, Woof!" went Fergus
as he hurried the animals outside.

Quickly, he switched off the television, washed the plates and had just finished tidying up when Farmer Bob's truck pulled into the yard.

"Phew! Just in time!" thought Fergus.
But had he forgotten anything? He tried
hard to remember. What about the cow . . .
. . . was she still in the bath?
Fergus groaned and closed his eyes.

The next thing he heard was
Farmer Bob's voice.
"Wake up Fergus. We're home!
Bet you've had a nice quiet day!"
"Humph!" thought Fergus.
"A quiet day be blowed!
It's been an upside-down day!"

But when he looked around the farm, everything seemed quite normal, and much to his surprise, the cow was back in the meadow.

Fergus gave a big sigh of relief.
"It must have been a dream after all!"
he thought.

. . . OR WAS IT!